Who Am I When
Nobody's Looking?

Loveland, Colorado

Christian Character Development Series:
Who Am I When Nobody's Looking?

Credits

Contributing Authors: Tim Baker, Mikal Keefer, Pamela J. Shoup, Helen Turnbull, and Paul Woods

Editor: Julie Meiklejohn

Creative Development Editors: Karl Leuthauser and Paul Woods

Chief Creative Officer: Joani Schultz

Copy Editor: Betty Taylor

Art Director: Kari K. Monson

Cover Art Director: Jeff A. Storm

Cover Designer and Artist: Alan Furst, Inc. Art and Design

Computer Graphic Artist: Pat Miller

Production Manager: Peggy Naylor

ISBN 0-7644-2128-X

Printed in the United States of America.

Contents

Introduction 4

How to Use This Book 4

Other Topics 6

The Studies

1. Avoiding the Tangled Web 7

   The Bible shows us how to live honest lives.

2. The Weight of Wisdom 14

   True wisdom comes from God.

3. When No One's Looking 21

   The Bible shows us the way to act with integrity.

4. He Will Lift You Up 28

   Jesus gives us the ultimate example of humility.

5. In God We Trust 36

   God wants us to trust in him for everything.

6. A Generous Spirit 43

   God shows us the way to be generous.

7. The Heart of Compassion .51

   The Bible shows us how to live compassionate lives.

8. *Semper Fidelis* (Always Faithful) 58

   God shows us how to live faithful lives.

Introduction

Our teenagers may be talking the talk, but are they walking the walk? Often an enormous gap exists between the Christian values many teenagers claim to have and their actions. Take a moment to ponder these sobering statistics:

• Six out of ten Christian teens say there is no such thing as absolute truth.

• One out of four denies the notion that acting in disobedience to God's laws brings about negative consequences.

• One-half believe the main purpose of life is enjoyment and personal fulfillment.

• Almost half contend that sometimes lying is necessary.

What's wrong with this picture?

Today's teenagers face more choices than any teenagers before them have. They must interpret, evaluate, and make moral decisions within a culture that ignores morality and changes rapidly. The choices your teenagers make today have eternal consequences. Can their faith keep up?

How can we help? We can begin by taking them on a journey—a journey toward stronger, more Christlike character. As teenagers learn to interpret and evaluate their decisions in light of their relationships with God, they will discover the importance of living out their faith in everything they do.

How to Use This Book

Who Am I When Nobody's Looking? contains eight studies, each designed to address a different aspect of personal character that teenagers will encounter.

• The study about **honesty** will help teenagers apply what the Bible says about being honest to their everyday lives.

• The study about **wisdom** will help students understand where true wisdom comes from and learn how to gain more of God's wisdom as they make decisions.

- The **integrity** study will help teenagers understand what integrity is and how it applies to their lives.

- The study about **humility** will show teenagers how to follow Christ's example of humility in everything they do.

- The study about **trust** gives students tools for turning everything in their lives over to God.

- The **generosity** study helps teenagers understand the type of generosity God wants from them.

- The study about **compassion** will help students realize the importance of compassion and will give them tools for showing compassion to others.

- The study about **faithfulness** will encourage students to act faithfully, no matter what they may be asked to do.

The Christian Character Development Series encourages students to examine their own character in a very individual, personal way. Each study in this series guides students to examine the topic individually, in pairs, and in larger groups.

Each study connects the topic and the Scriptures to God-centered character development—the idea that God gives us a model of quality character in his Word, as well as a desire to know him and to become more like him.

Each person in your group (including you) will have his or her own book to use extensively throughout each study for journaling and other writing and drawing activities. Each study begins with a section called "Read About It" and then follows with a section called "Write About It." These sections provide teenagers with "food for thought" about the topic and provide the opportunity to respond to those thoughts, right in their books. You may choose to have your students complete these sections before your group meets, or you may decide to have students complete these sections at the beginning of your meeting time.

Other sections of the book are designed so students can work through them with a minimum of direction from you. Any direction you may need to give your students is included in the "Leaders Instructions" boxes. You're encouraged to participate and learn right along with the students—your insights will enhance students' learning.

Each study provides a combination of introspective, active, and interactive learning. Teenagers learn best by experiencing the topic they're learning about and then sharing their thoughts and reactions with others.

The Christian Character Development Series will help you guide your teenagers through the perils and pitfalls of growing up in today's culture. Use the studies in this book to work with your youth to understand what it means to have high standards of character and to learn why character is important to God.

Other Topics

Who Am I With Others?

Knowing God

Conflict

Forgiveness

Friendship

Parents and Other Authorities

Dating

Loneliness

Love

Who Am I to God?

Salvation

The Bible

The Trinity

Prayer

Service

Faith

Sharing Faith

Worship

Who Am I...Really?

Righteousness

Popularity

Success

Self-Esteem

The Family of God

Spiritual Gifts

Role Models and Heroes

The Future

Who Am I Inside?

Hope

Fear

Guilt

Pride

Joy

Grief

Anger

Peace

Who Am I to Judge?

Sex

Drugs and Alcohol

Peer Pressure

Moral Absolutes

Idolatry

Media and Music

Handling Stress

Making Good Decisions

Avoiding the Tangled Web

 ## The Bible shows us how to live honest lives.

Supplies: You'll need Bibles, pens or pencils, Bible concordances, a skein of yarn, and scissors.

Preparation: On a table, set out the supplies to use during the study.

Leader Instructions

Begin by having students each read the "Read About It" section and respond in the "Write About It" section.

Read About It

According to an article in USA Weekend, "the American leaders of the new millennium—today's teenagers—are increasingly willing to lie, steal and cheat their way through life."

A survey of ten thousand high school students by the Josephson Institute of Ethics shows the following:

- 46 percent of teenagers say they have stolen something from a store,
- 70 percent say they have cheated on an exam, and
- 92 percent say they have lied to a parent.

Those students who said religion was very important to them were not much more honest. Sixty-nine percent of them admitted to cheating on exams.

So what does the Bible have to say about honesty? It clearly tells us to lead honest lives. Exodus 20:1 says, "And God spoke all these words" to Moses in giving him the Ten Commandments, including "You shall not give false testimony against your neighbor" (Exodus 20:16).

False testimony. Lies. They come from the "evil one," Jesus says in Matthew 5:37. One of our goals as Christians is to be like Jesus, and that means living honestly and with integrity.

Write About It

- Do you think teenagers are as dishonest as this survey implies? Why or why not?

_____

_____

_____

- On a scale from one to five, rank how honest you are. (Five means you are totally honest in all that you do.) Why did you choose the number you did?

_____

_____

_____

- Think about some times you haven't been honest. List those below. (If you gave yourself a five above, think about your feelings and whether you are being honest with yourself.)

_____

_____

_____

- Read Matthew 5:34-37. What do you think this means? How can you conduct yourself so your "yes" means yes and your "no" means no?

_____

_____

_____

Experience It

Extension Idea

If you have time, have each group also create its own situation about honesty and then create individual and group responses.

Leader Instructions

Have students form four groups, and point out the supply table you've prepared before the study. To each group, assign one of the situations on the "What Would You Do?" page (p. 9). If you have a class of fifteen or more, form eight groups and assign two groups to each situation.

In your group, follow the instructions on the "What Would You Do?" page (p. 9). Use the supplies on the supply table as needed.

What Would You Do?

Think about your assigned situation, discuss it with your group, and then write an individual response. When everyone in your group has finished, work together to create a group response that everyone can endorse. After you've finished, work with your group to complete the instructions in the last paragraph of the page.

Situation 1

 White lies or half-truths are OK if you're trying to protect someone's feelings or to be tactful. Do you agree or disagree?

angry

Situation 2

As your team heads into the state championship game, winning is everything. But referees aren't perfect, and they sometimes make bad calls. If the referee makes a wrong call involving you, in your favor, during the biggest game of your life, should you say something? Why or why not?

Situation 3

"Forays into misbehavior are how children—even the best-raised ones—learn about right and wrong. All children will push the envelope now and again; it's one way they learn about limits. 'To expect a child to never lie or steal is probably not realistic or even necessarily desirable from a developmental point of view.' " *(James Nickel, University of Colorado, quoted in The Denver Post, October 21, 1998)* Do you agree or disagree? Why?

Situation 4

You find a paper bag containing a large amount of cash with no indication of where it came from. Do you turn it in to authorities, or do you keep it? Why?

Using a Bible concordance, find a reference to honesty or being honest in the Bible, and write out that Scripture and reference here:

find verse for meditation - honesty

What about when its hard...

Leader Instructions

When groups have finished, have a spokesperson from each group share the situation and the group response. If the entire group cannot endorse one team statement, have the spokesperson explain why. Also have each group share its chosen Scripture.

After groups have finished, process the experience using questions such as these:

- *Is it ever OK to not be completely honest? Explain.*
- *Do you think there might be degrees of honesty, ranging from a half-truth to perjury? Explain.*
- *What does Scripture say about honesty?*
- *What does being honest say about your character?*

Now have students sit in two lines, facing each other, and give the skein of yarn to a person on one end.

When you have the yarn, say a truthful statement about yourself, and then toss the yarn to the person sitting across from you while you continue to hold on to the end of the yarn. (Your truthful statement can be anything you choose to say, such as "I am sixteen," "I love my family," or "I'm not very good in math.")

Be sure to keep the yarn taut, and continue saying truthful statements and tossing the yarn until everyone has had an opportunity to speak.

When you've finished, observe the neat pattern of straight lines you've created. Now you'll see what lies can do to the pattern. Continue to hold on to your original piece of yarn. When you have caught the yarn again, make an untruthful statement about yourself, and then toss the yarn randomly to any other person in the two lines. When everyone has finished, the pattern should look like a tangled web.

Now observe your tangled web. Perhaps you've heard the saying, "Oh, what a tangled web we weave, when first we practice to deceive!" Discuss these questions as a whole group:

- How is this tangled web like telling lies?
- What happens when you continue to tell one lie after another?
- Is it possible to untangle this kind of web to discover the truth underneath? If so, how?

Tell Me More...

"A liar should have a good memory."—Folklore advice, as quoted in *A Treasury of Jewish Folklore*

truthful *humble* *strong conscience* *Holy Spirit*
communicative *courageous* *realistic* *wise*

Leader Instructions

If students can't think of good ideas for untangling the web, cut through the yarn with a pair of scissors and tell them that sometimes you have to "cut through" lies and deception to see the truth.

Ask two volunteers to read aloud Proverbs 12:19 and Proverbs 24:26. Then discuss this question as a whole group:

- *What do you think these words of wisdom mean?*

Apply It

Find a partner. Together, make a list of people you both perceive as honest people. These can be people you know well or public or historical figures. After each name, tell why you think that person is honest or what he or she does or says to present him or herself as an honest person.

Capla - tells wise truth   Saval - humble

Mom - not doing wrong

Glen - truth hurts

When you've finished, find another pair and share your lists.

As a foursome, list about ten character traits of honest people, such as dependability or trustworthiness.

Then brainstorm some benefits of being an honest person, and list those here.

Read Colossians 3:8-10 with your group, and then discuss what you think is meant by "old self" and "new self." Write some of your group's thoughts here:

Now on your own, think of a commitment you'll make to take one action that will demonstrate your own "new self." You might vow not to partake in gossip or choose to be completely honest for one whole day.

Extension Idea

Have students create their own honesty quiz to share with friends and family. Have them make a list of ten situations involving honest or dishonest behavior and add three different behavior choices for each question ("a," "b," and "c"). Pair each honest answer with the same letter.

Here's a sample question with possible answers:

- *Would you keep the extra money if a clerk in a store undercharged you?*

  a. *Yes, if I could get away with it.*

  b. *Yes, but only at a large chain store that wouldn't miss the money.*

  c. *No, I would always tell a clerk if I noticed a mistake.*

Score the quiz by saying something like this: "If you selected eight or more 'c' answers, you're an honest person living by biblical standards. If you chose four to seven 'c' answers, examine your behavior and yourself. If you selected fewer than four 'c' answers, check the length of your nose, Pinocchio!"

(Remember the Jim Carrey movie *Liar, Liar* in which the main character couldn't tell a lie—at all?)

On the drawing of the paper person below, write "My New Self." Then write your commitment to being honest on your paper person. Share your commitment with your original partner, and take a minute or two to pray for each other. Make a plan to hold your partner accountable throughout the next week by contacting him or her at least once about this commitment.

Live It

Read Psalm 112. Then ask yourself the following questions, and respond in the spaces provided:

• The psalm describes a person who will demonstrate God's blessing by being righteous, compassionate, gracious, having a steadfast heart, trusting in the Lord, and having fear of the Lord. Do you see any of these qualities in yourself? How could you demonstrate more of these qualities?

_____

_____

• The psalm says a righteous man will be remembered forever. How would you like to be remembered after you've gone?

_____

_____

• The psalm talks about the punishment of a wicked man. Do you ever feel wicked when you gossip or tell a lie? How can you avoid those actions in the future?

_____

_____

Tell Me More...

Of any story you tell, the truth is always the easiest version to remember. Can you think of a time you told a small lie or passed on untrue gossip, and it blew up in your face? It might have left you feeling really ashamed of yourself. How many times have you said something and then wished you hadn't said it? Sometimes we need to pray before we speak. Daily ask God to help you speak only the truth and to speak always with integrity. Strive to demonstrate the kind of character that you admire in others. A good Scripture to help keep you on track in your daily life is Philippians 4:8.

Tell Me More...

There are lots of stories in history about the honesty of famous people, such as "Honest Abe" Lincoln and George Washington. Remember the story about George Washington and the cherry tree? Young George was given a hatchet, and he liked to chop on various things with it. One day George's father discovered that the bark on his cherry tree was all chopped up. (George didn't actually chop the tree down, but he did kill it.) George admitted to the deed, saying, "I can't tell a lie, Pa."

Ironically, according to *The Book of Lies* by M. Hirsh Goldberg, the Washington story is most likely a fabrication by a nineteenth-century biographer named Mason Weems. It didn't even appear until the fifth edition of his book about George Washington in 1806!

Despite this famous story, history remembers Washington as a good and honest man. What a great way to be remembered!

Later in his life, Washington said, "I hope I shall possess firmness and virtue enough to maintain what I consider the most enviable of all titles, the character of an honest man."

The Weight of Wisdom

 **True wisdom comes from God.**

Supplies: You'll need Bibles; pens or pencils; Bible concordances (optional); and various craft supplies such as tape, construction paper, paper cups, pipe cleaners, modeling clay, craft sticks, and scissors.

Preparation: On a table, set out the supplies to use during the study.

Leader Instructions

Begin by having students each read the "Read About It" section and respond in the "Write About It" section.

Read About It

Share everything.

Play fair.

Don't hit people.

Put things back where you found them.

Clean up your own mess.

Don't take things that aren't yours.

Say you're sorry when you hurt somebody.

Wash your hands before you eat.

Flush.

Warm cookies and cold milk are good for you.

Live a balanced life—learn some and think some and draw and paint and sing and dance and play and work every day some.

Take a nap every afternoon.

When you go out into the world, watch out for traffic, hold hands, and stick together.

(Robert Fulghum, *All I Really Need to Know I Learned in Kindergarten*)

Write About It

- Place a check mark ✔ next to each of the previous statements that might be wisdom from God, and place a star ☆ next to each statement that might be wisdom from the world. Can you tell the difference between the two? If so, how?

_____

_____

_____

- What does wisdom look like? Draw a picture of it below.

- What do you think makes a person wise?

_____

_____

_____

- Read Job 28:20-28. What does this passage tell you about the origin of wisdom?

_____

_____

Experience It

Leader Instructions

Have students form four groups, and point out the supply table you've prepared before the study.

In your group, follow the instructions on the "Perfect Wisdom" page (p. 16). Use the supplies on the supply table as needed.

Extension Idea

For Section 3, consider having groups write stories based on the life of Solomon. Have them include the knowledge that 1 Kings 4:29-34 mentions, as well as other information that might not be included in the Bible account.

Perfect Wisdom

Section 1

Read 1 Kings 3:1-15. As a group, discuss the following questions and write the answers in the spaces provided:

• If God told you that he'd give you anything you wanted, what would you ask for? Why?

_____

_____

• What does this passage reveal about the importance of wisdom?

_____

_____

Using the craft supplies provided, create your own piece of art that represents the wisdom the world might seek. You might create something that represents wealth, status, or education. When you've created your object, share it with the other members of your group. Then discuss the following questions in your group, and write the responses in the spaces provided:

• What's the difference between wisdom and education? Do you think wisdom is more important? Why?

_____

_____

• Why should we seek God's wisdom?

_____

_____

• If you were able to have God's wisdom, how important do you think wealth, power, and beauty would be to you? Explain.

_____

_____

Section 2

Read 1 Kings 3:16-28. As a group, discuss the following questions and write the answers in the spaces provided:

• How do you know Solomon used wisdom from God?

_____

_____

• If Solomon had used worldly wisdom, how might he have solved this problem?

_____

_____

Draw a line down the center of the following space.

Write "Worldly Wisdom" on one side and "God's Wisdom" on the other side. Work with your group to make a chart that compares the differences between worldly wisdom and God's wisdom. List ways each type of wisdom is distinct from the other. For example, a distinguishing characteristic of God's wisdom is that it comes from God. A characteristic of worldly wisdom is that it tends to ignore God. You'll end up with a chart of words and phrases that compares and contrasts the differences between the two types of wisdom. You might want to search the concordances to help you gain a better understanding of what God's wisdom is. When you've finished, discuss these questions in your group and write the answers in the spaces provided:

• What differences did you notice between worldly wisdom and God's wisdom?

_____

_____

• Do you think God's wisdom is necessary only for people who make "important" decisions, or is it necessary for everyone? Why?

_____

_____

Section 3

Read 1 Kings 4:29-34. As a group, discuss the following questions and write the answers in the spaces provided:
• This passage describes the depth and breadth of Solomon's wisdom. What does this passage say about the importance of using the wisdom God has given us?

_____

_____

• What's one trait you notice in yourself that causes you to say, "Hey! I'm a wise person"? What makes you notice that you need to keep seeking more wisdom?

_____

_____

• What are some ways we can use God's wisdom to help our friends? our families? the church?

_____

_____

On your own, write a one-sentence prayer asking God for wisdom. Include a reason you think you need wisdom, or include what you would use wisdom for if God gave it to you. After you've written your prayer, get together with your group and combine your sentence prayers into one large group prayer. When you've combined your prayers, spend time praying through the prayer as a group. When you've finished praying, answer the following question on your own and then discuss your answer with your group.
• Once you're convinced that God has given you wisdom, what is the best thing to do (check one)?
Be bold, and go out to test it. ___
Keep it to myself, and wait for a situation in which I can use it. ___
Forget about it. ___
Explain your choice to your group.

Leader Instructions

Apply It

On your own, read through the passages on the "Prayers for Wisdom" page (p. 20). When you've read through the passages, think about ways the passages can apply to your life and spend some time completing the sections of the sheet about relationships, schoolwork, and walking with God. Once you've completed the page, find a partner and share your responses with him or her. Then complete the "Please pray..." section of the page on your own. For each of the "Please pray..." sections, write some specific ways your partner can pray for you to gain wisdom in each of these areas. When you've finished writing in this section, exchange books with your partner and write down his or her prayer requests in the margin of your book so you'll remember to pray specifically for your partner's requests.

When you've finished writing your partner's requests in your book, spend some time in prayer for each other, including the requests you recorded.

Tell Me More...

When the Old Testament speaks about wisdom, it implies far more than we might expect.

The Hebrew words for wisdom used predominantly in Old Testament literature are the words "hakam" and "hokmah." These words suggest more than just obtaining knowledge. They imply the marriage of several key concepts including being sensitive to God, willingly subjecting ourselves to him, and applying divine guidelines to everyday situations. Wisdom is found and demonstrated by taking what Jesus said and combining it with our everyday experiences.

(Lawrence O. Richards, *Zondervan Expository Dictionary of Bible Words*)

So how can you "get wise"? Ask God for wisdom. Talk to people. Ask for their opinions. Listen to people who have lived through a variety of circumstances. Read books by people who are sought after for their perspective, honesty, and spiritual depth.

Live It

When you have some spare time, complete this section on your own.

- What will you do to acquire wisdom over the next few weeks?

_____

_____

- Read 1 Corinthians 3:18-20. In what areas of your life do you need to become "foolish" in order to gain wisdom?

_____

_____

_____

- Spend time this week praying for wisdom. Write things you notice as you're praying.

_____

_____

_____

- Who can you talk to about gaining wisdom? Seek out these people, and ask them to give you advice about being a wise person. Ask them to tell you about their lives and their pursuit of wisdom.

_____

_____

_____

Tell Me More...

Picture this. An old man sits cross-legged on a rock jutting out over the ocean. His face is unusually peaceful. This man might be considered the perfect picture of wisdom.

This picture of wisdom stands in direct contrast to what the Bible tells us wisdom is. Consider these passages from God's Word:

"The fear of the Lord is the beginning of wisdom" (Psalm 111:10a).

"Wisdom is found in those who take advice" (Proverbs 13:10b).

"The lips of the wise spread knowledge" (Proverbs 15:7a).

The Bible paints a picture of wisdom different from the world's picture. A wise person isn't removed from society. Wisdom doesn't necessarily mean keeping your mouth shut. And, most of all, wisdom is found through the fear and respect of the Creator of the universe. If you want, you can go sit on a rock and stare into space. But you'll probably end up daydreaming rather than gaining any wisdom.

Prayers for Wisdom

• Wisdom in my relationships: Proverbs 2:8-20; Proverbs 27:9-10; and Philippians 2:19-30.

Please pray...

• Wisdom in my schoolwork: Ephesians 4:11-13 and Colossians 3:16-17, 23-24.

Please pray...

• Wisdom in my walk with God: Psalm 119:68, 73; and Ephesians 3:14-19.

Please pray...

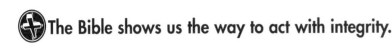

When No One's Looking

✜ **The Bible shows us the way to act with integrity.**

Supplies: You'll need Bibles, pens or pencils, a painting or photograph with significant detail, paper, and markers.

Preparation: On a table, set out the supplies to use during the study.

Leader Instructions

Begin by having students each read the "Read About It" section and respond in the "Write About It" section.

Read About It

Last week I read about a woman, apparently pregnant, who walked out of the grocery store. Suspicious, the assistant manager stopped her. She later "gave birth" to a pound of butter, a chuck roast, a bottle of pancake syrup, two tubes of toothpaste, hair tonic, and several bars of candy.

One estimate says that one out of every fifty-two customers every day carries away at least one unpaid-for item.

Now let's remember that shoplifting is merely one thin slice of humanity's stale cake of dishonesty. Don't forget our depraved track record: cheating on exams, taking a towel from the hotel, not working a full eight hours, bold-face lies and half truths...

The answer, simplistic though it may seem, is a return to honesty. Integrity may be an even better word. It would be a tough reversal for some...but oh, how needed! It boils down to an internal decision. Nothing less will counteract dishonesty. External punishment may hurt, but it doesn't solve.

(Charles Swindoll, *The Quest for Character*)

Write About It

• What is integrity? Write your definition below.

_____

_____

_____

- How would you respond to the statement that integrity "boils down to an internal decision"?

_____

_____

_____

- What do you think motivates a person to make internal decisions that demonstrate integrity?

_____

_____

_____

- Read Hebrews 4:12-14. What does this passage have to do with integrity?

_____

_____

_____

- Think about your personal integrity level. Then mark where you'd put yourself on the continuum below. Explain why you placed your mark where you did.

Steve Scumball   Jennifer Jerk   Joe Average   Gloria Good   Ivan Integrity
⊢————————+————————+————————+————————⊣

_____

_____

_____

- Read Hebrews 4:15-16. According to these verses, what hope do we have when we fail in our quest for integrity?

_____

_____

_____

Experience It

Leader Instructions

On a separate sheet of paper, draw as complete a reproduction as possible of the picture you just saw. Use whatever supplies are available. When your time is up, share your picture with the rest of the class.

Provide art supplies, and allow students to get really creative.

Leader Instructions

Give students about five minutes to draw.

Form groups of about four. In your group, read James 1:22-24. Then discuss the following questions. After each question, share your conclusions with the rest of the class.

• What do you think James is getting at in this passage?

_____

_____

_____

Tell Me More...

"Almost all of us live two lives: what people see outside and what is really going on inside. In school we learn what outward signs of attention will please the teacher. At a job we learn to "put up a good front" whenever the boss happens to stroll by. As if donning masks, we style our hair, choose our clothes, and use body language to impress those around us. Over time, we learn to excel at hiding truly serious problems.

"People tend to judge by outward appearances and so can easily be fooled. Acquaintances are often shocked when a mass-murderer is arrested. 'He seemed like such a nice man!' they insist. The outside appearance did not match the inside reality.

"[Matthew] chapters 5–7 announce that the time has come for us to change not just the outside, but the inside. In Jesus' day, religious people tried to impress each other with showy outward behavior. They wore gaunt and hungry looks during a brief fast, prayed grandiosely if people were watching, and went so far as to wear Bible verses strapped to their foreheads and left arms.

"In his famous Sermon on the Mount, Jesus blasts the hypocrisy behind such seemingly harmless practices. God is not fooled by appearances. We cannot fake behavior to impress him. He knows that inside the best of us lurk dark thoughts of hatred, pride, and lust—internal problems only he can deal with."

(The Student Bible)

• How does James' message relate to living with integrity?

_____

_____

_____

• How was the drawing experience similar to what's described in this passage? How was it different?

_____

_____

_____

• Do you think your drawing looks like the original? Why?

_____

_____

_____

Leader Instructions

Assign one of the following passages to each of your groups: James 1:25-27 and Mark 12:28-34. After each question, have students report on the insights found in their passages.

In your group, study your assigned passage and answer the questions on the following page:

Tell Me More...

"People often think of Christian morality as a kind of bargain in which God says, 'If you keep a lot of rules I'll reward you, and if you don't I'll do the other thing.' I do not think that is the best way of looking at it. I would much rather say that every time you make a choice you are turning the central part of you, the part of you that chooses, into something a little different from what it was before. And taking your life as a whole, with all your innumerable choices, all your life long you are slowly turning this central thing either into a heavenly creature or into a hellish creature: either into a creature that is in harmony with God, and with other creatures, and with itself, or else into one that is in a state of war and hatred with God, and with its fellow-creatures, and with itself…Each of us at each moment is progressing to the one state or the other. "

(C.S. Lewis, *Mere Christianity*)

- How could you have done better with your drawing?

_____

_____

- According to your passage, how can we do better in living lives of integrity?

_____

_____

_____

- What does your passage say about what God expects of us?

_____

_____

_____

Apply It

We've seen that the Bible shows us the way to act with integrity. Now let's apply that to real life. Below, write a situation in which someone has to make a choice between something attractive and acting with integrity. For example, you might create a situation in which a friend asks you to lie to his mom to convince her that he was with you and not out drinking on Friday night. Try to write your situation so that the choice isn't easy or obvious, and make the situation something you or your friends might face. You'll be sharing your situation with others who will discuss the situation and the choices.

_____

_____

_____

Leader Instructions

Give students about five minutes to write their situations.

After five minutes, join about three others to make a group. One at a time, share your situations. Discuss the following questions for each situation, and jot down the group's conclusions.

• What makes this choice difficult?

_____

_____

_____

• Why is making the choice of integrity a good idea in this situation?

_____

_____

_____

Leader Instructions

After groups have discussed the questions for all the situations in their group, have each group share one or two of its situations with the class. Ask groups to choose situations that are closest to situations they might actually face. When all groups have shared, have students form pairs.

Tell your partner which of the situations might be most difficult for you and why. Then look back at James 1:22-27 and Mark 12:28-34 to discover ways to act with integrity even in the most difficult situations. Write those ideas below:

_____

_____

_____

Below, write one word that symbolizes a challenge you face or know you may face in living a life of integrity. Make sure it's a word you wouldn't mind mentioning aloud.

_____

Leader Instructions

When students have each written a word, form a circle and close the study with prayer. Begin with the following prayer starter: "God, thank you for showing us the way to act with integrity. Help us to maintain integrity in the areas of...

Let students say their words aloud, one at a time. Then finish the prayer with something like, "Thank you, God. Amen."

Live It

- Think of a person you know who lacks integrity. List things about him or her that give you that impression.

_____

_____

- Examine yourself to see if any of those things apply to your own behavior, then read Hebrews 4:15-16. Think about how you might avoid becoming like the person you identified in the last question. Journal your thoughts below.

_____

_____

_____

- Think of a person you know who demonstrates integrity. List things about him or her that give you that impression.

_____

_____

_____

- Think about how you might seek to become more like that person. Read Matthew 6:19-21 for some additional ideas. Journal your thoughts below.

_____

_____

_____

Tell Me More...

"It is easier to fight for one's principles than to live up to them."

—Alfred Adler

He Will Lift You Up

 Jesus gives us the ultimate example of humility.

Supplies: You'll need Bibles, pens or pencils, an old towel, paper, inexpensive watercolor sets with paintbrushes, and markers.

Preparation: On a table, set out the supplies to use during the study.

Leader Instructions

Begin by having students each read the "Read About It" section and respond in the "Write About It" section.

Read About It

Christ's attitude was simple. Jesus saw the fallen, rebellious condition of mankind and then did everything necessary to redeem the world. Although the world deserved judgment, he did not come to judge the world, but to save it... The Son of God saw the need of the world and emptied himself to meet it. He gave up all that was his in the Godhead: His privileges, powers and position as the very form of God. Being found in appearance as a man, he humbled himself, remaining obedient to death, thus securing our eternal redemption. This is the mind that we are to have in us "which was also in Christ Jesus."

Out of the nature of selfless love emerges the mind of Christ.

(Francis Frangipane, "Possessing the Mind of Christ to See as Jesus Sees," Advancing Church Ministries, www.frangipane.org/article/mind.html)

Write About It

• What does the word "humility" mean to you?

_____

_____

_____

• Write about a time you've experienced someone else's Christlike behavior.

_____

_____

_____

- Do you think that behavior was an act of humility? Explain.

_____

_____

- Read the "Tell Me More..." box in the margin. Do William Temple's words change or reflect your definition of humility? Explain.

_____

_____

- Find a partner, and work together to write a definition for each of the following words. You can write dictionary-style definitions or define the words by example. For example, you might describe "shame" as David's feeling of guilt for what he'd done to Bathsheba and Uriah, or you might describe "modesty" as not drawing attention to oneself.

pride _____

low self-esteem _____

high self-esteem _____

self-centeredness _____

shame _____

selfishness _____

selflessness _____

vanity _____

meekness _____

modesty _____

self-effacement _____

Tell Me More...

"Humility does not mean thinking less of yourself than of other people, nor does it mean having a low opinion of your own gifts. It means freedom from thinking about yourself one way or the other at all...The humility which consists in being a great deal occupied about yourself, and saying you are of little worth, is not Christian humility. It is one form of self-occupation and a very poor and futile one at that."

(William Temple, *Christ in his Church,* quoted in *The Book of Wisdom*)

Leader Instructions

After pairs have finished, have the whole group answer the following questions:

- *Which of the words you've defined are similar to "humility"?*
- *Which words are opposites of "humility"?*
- *Which words could you use to describe Jesus?*
- *Using the words you've defined, fill in the blank to make this a true statement: "I can have _____ and be humble at the same time."*

Experience It

Leader Instructions

Have students sit in a circle on the floor with their feet out. Ask a volunteer to read aloud John 13:1-17. Then use the old towel to wipe the shoes of everyone in the circle. Kneel as you do this, and be sure to encourage a reflective atmosphere. When you've finished, direct the group to continue the study in their books.

Extension Idea

For extra impact, tear the towel into strips and give a strip to each student to take home as a reminder of Christ's servanthood and humility. You may also want to consider conducting an actual foot-washing service with your students.

On your own, journal your response to this question:

• What thoughts or feelings did you have as the leader washed your feet? What thoughts or feelings do you think the disciples must have had as their Lord and Savior washed their feet?

_____

_____

_____

Carefully read the following statements on your own, and decide whether you think they're true or false. Be prepared to explain why you chose each of your answers.

	True	False
I have to be humble *really* only before God.	❏	❏
Humility is not something God can teach me.	❏	❏
Being humble means being a doormat.	❏	❏
I can't *learn* how to be humble.	❏	❏
Humility only comes from asking forgiveness.	❏	❏
I can't be humble and have good self-esteem.	❏	❏
I can't be humble without having low self-esteem.	❏	❏
I don't have to be humble toward people I don't like.	❏	❏
I can't be humble toward people I don't love.	❏	❏
I can't be as humble as Jesus.	❏	❏
I can't be humble all the time.	❏	❏
Humility comes from grace.	❏	❏

Find a partner, and discuss your answers. Then together reread John 13:1-17. With your partner, look through the passage to find verses that might be good responses to the true/false statements above. Write those verse numbers next to the appropriate statements.

Discuss these questions with your partner:

- What acts of humility did Jesus perform in this Scripture?
- How is Jesus' humility different from yours? How is it the same?
- How does knowing God can be humble before you change the way you think about your own humility?

Jesus didn't wash your feet. But he serves you. How does (or did) he serve you? Read John 17:20-25.

Jesus knew he was going to be arrested. Yet his *last* act as a free man was to pray for us. Name some other ways Jesus has served you:

_____

_____

_____

Discuss these questions with your partner:

- How was Jesus' prayer for us an act of humility?
- How was Jesus' death an act of humility?

Apply It

Choose a quote or a motto that best describes how you feel about being humble. You may use one of the quotes from the "Tell Me More…" box on pages 34-35 or come up with your own. With the watercolors, paint something on a piece of paper that reflects humility. It could be a portrait of a humble person you know, an element of God's creation that reminds you of his control and glory, or a scene depicting the time in your life you've felt the most humble. When your artwork dries, write your motto on it. Explain to the class what your picture and your motto say about your humility.

Leader Instructions

To close the meeting, collect all the books and redistribute them so that everyone has someone else's book. Have the class turn to this page.

Write a short prayer of humility for the person who owns this book so that he or she can remember to be humble before God and before others. You might write something like this:

"Father, I thank you for sending your Son to us so that I can know what humility is. I pray that I can share with others the selfless love that is a natural extension of being humble before God."

_____

_____

_____

_____

Leader Instructions

When the students have written their prayers, have them return the books to their owners. Close in prayer by asking each person to read aloud the prayer of humility written in his or her book.

Live It

Every day for the next week, complete one of the following exercises. Before you end the day, write a short journal entry about what you've experienced.

Day 1

Make a note of every example of God's miracles you see today. Do those miracles make you feel humble? Explain how you expressed your humility before God.

_____

_____

_____

Day 2

Sometime today, during a moment of tension, anger, fear, danger, hesitation, or exhaustion, hand your problem over to God. Explain how (or if) you felt humble in the presence of God's control.

_____

_____

_____

Tell Me More...

Mother Teresa lived every day of her life in humility. But even though she spent her life working with the most destitute of people, she learned that the poorest people could share with her the greatest moments of humility. In one incident, Mother Teresa and some of her fellow sisters took in some people who were left to die in the streets of Calcutta. Mother Teresa personally took care of one woman who was much worse than the others. She took the woman's hand, and the woman looked up at Mother Teresa and simply said, "Thank you." Then she died. This is Mother Teresa's response:

"I could not help but examine my conscience before her. I asked, 'What would I say if I were in her place?' And my answer was very simple. I would have tried to draw a little attention to myself. I would have said, 'I am hungry, I am dying, I am cold, I am in pain,' or something like that. But she gave me much more—she gave me her grateful love. And she died with a smile on her face."

(excerpted from Mother Teresa's "1994 Address to the National Prayer Breakfast")

The greatest caches of humility—moments of unconditional, selfless love—often come from the people who seem to have nothing.

Day 3

Look into the face of everyone you encounter today, and imagine you're staring into the face of Christ. Explain how humility might have changed (or did change) the way you react to others.

Day 4

Notice every time you receive communication today—every phone call, e-mail, conversation, letter, CD, TV show, or book. Think of each piece of information you received as a gift. Explain the humility you feel after receiving so many gifts in one day.

Day 5

Who do you feel superior to and why? Take five minutes out of each hour today to pray for that person. Explain how humility through prayer makes you feel and how you think it makes God feel.

_____

_____

_____

_____

Day 6

What can you give up today? a bus seat? a place in line at the store? time for a friend?

Who did you give something to? Explain how you feel when you offer something. Do you feel humble? Why or why not?

_____

_____

_____

_____

Day 7

God is all-powerful, yet he chooses to serve you. He comforts _you;_ he cares for _you;_ he loves _you._ How is God serving you today? Do you feel humbled by God's love? Explain.

_____

_____

_____

_____

Tell Me More...

"Humble yourselves before the Lord, and he will lift you up" (James 4:10).

"As the nightingale instinctively flees from the sound of the hawk, so does the beauty of humility vanish in the presence of pride" (William A. Ward, quoted in _Sensible Sayings and Wacky Wit_ by Vern McLellan).

"For whoever exalts himself will be humbled, and whoever humbles himself will be exalted" (Matthew 23:12).

"Don't be humble; you're not that great" (Golda Meir, quoted in _Sensible Sayings and Wacky Wit_ by Vern McLellan).

"Your beginnings will seem humble, so prosperous will your future be" (Job 8:7).

"God created the world out of nothing, and as long as we are nothing, he can make something out of us" (Martin Luther, quoted in *Sensible Sayings and Wacky Wit* by Vern McLellan).

"He guides the humble in what is right and teaches them his way" (Psalm 25:9).

"I believe the first test of a truly great man is his humility" (John Ruskin, quoted in *Sensible Sayings and Wacky Wit* by Vern McLellan).

"It is my chief duty to accomplish humble tasks as though they were great and noble" (Helen Keller, quoted in *Sensible Sayings and Wacky Wit* by Vern McLellan).

"And those who walk in pride he is able to humble" (Daniel 4:37b).

"I'll just have to save him. Because, after all, a person's a person, no matter how small" (Horton the elephant, from *Horton Hears a Who!* by Dr. Seuss).

"Be completely humble and gentle; be patient, bearing with one another in love" (Ephesians 4:2).

"True love is but a humble, low-born thing" (James Russell Lowell, "Love," quoted in *The Book of Wisdom*).

In God We Trust

 God wants us to trust in him for everything.

Supplies: You'll need Bibles, pens or pencils, colored markers, newsprint, tape, and concordances (optional).

Preparation: On a table, set out the supplies to use during the study.

Leader Instructions

Begin by having students each read the "Read About It" section and respond in the "Write About It" section.

Read About It

"In God we trust." It's a principle America was founded on and a basic foundation of our Christian faith. Trust in God. Have faith.

Just look at some of the great faith heroes of the Bible. God told Joshua to march around Jericho for six days with his army and seven priests carrying trumpets and rams' horns in front of the Ark of the Covenant. On the seventh day, the priests were to blow the trumpets and all the people were to give a loud shout. Then the walls of Jericho would collapse and Joshua's army would conquer. Joshua's army and the priests followed God's direction, and it happened—just as God promised. If you were an army general, would you consider these sound military tactics?

God told Abraham to sacrifice his son, Isaac, as a burnt offering. Just as Abraham was about to slay his son with a knife, God stopped him. Because Abraham passed this test of faith, God rewarded him by making his descendants "as numerous as the stars in the sky and as the sand on the seashore" (Genesis 22:17b). Could you sacrifice someone you love if God asked you to?

It was tough to convince Moses that he could free his people, but he trusted in the power of God to bring plagues to Egypt and to part the Red Sea. Moses went on to defeat Pharaoh and lead the Israelites out of bondage and into the Promised Land.

Could you do the same? Could you trust God enough to do his will, no matter what your eyes or your ears or your brain were telling you to do differently?

"Trust in the Lord with all your heart and lean not on your own understanding; in all your ways acknowledge him, and he will make your paths straight" (Proverbs 3:5-6).

Write About It

• Can you think of a time God asked you to do something that seemed impossible? How did you respond?

_____

_____

• In which areas of your life do you need to trust in God more? Explain.

_____

_____

• How could you show God that you trust him to guide you?

_____

_____

• Read Matthew 6:25-34. What do you think this Scripture really says? If you "seek first his kingdom and his righteousness" as this Scripture says, how might this help you trust in God to take care of everything else in your life?

_____

Tell Me More...

When life's burdens seem really heavy, remember this story and trust that God is in charge.

The young man was at the end of his rope. Seeing no way out, he dropped to his knees in prayer. "Lord, I can't go on," he said. "I have too heavy a cross to bear." The Lord replied, "My son, if you can't bear its weight, just place your cross inside this room. Then, open that other door, and pick out any cross you wish."

The man was filled with relief. "Thank you, Lord," he sighed, and he did as he was told. Upon entering the other door, he saw many crosses, some so large the tops were not visible. Then he saw a tiny cross leaning against a far wall. "I'd like that one, Lord," he whispered. And the Lord replied, "My son, that is the cross you just brought in."

(Creators Syndicate Inc.)

Experience It

Leader Instructions

Divide your class into four groups, and explain that the class will be creating a Trust Web. Distribute a differently colored marker to each group, and assign groups each a section from the "Trust Web" page (pp. 38-39).

While groups work, write "Trust in God" in large letters in the middle of a large sheet of newsprint and tape the newsprint to the wall.

In your group, follow the instructions on the "Trust Web" page (p. 38).

Trust Web

Follow the directions for your assigned group.

Group 1

Brainstorm a list of times we need to trust in God. Choose one volunteer to write your group's list to the right of the central idea on the newsprint sheet.

Group 2

Brainstorm a list of ways you can show your trust in God. Then choose one volunteer to write your group's list to the left of the central idea on the newsprint sheet.

Group 3

Brainstorm a list of reasons we know God is trustworthy. Then choose one volunteer to write your group's list above the central idea on the newsprint sheet.

Group 4

Brainstorm a list of Bible characters (or people you know) who trusted (or trust) in God. Then choose one volunteer to write your group's list below the central idea on the newsprint sheet.

All Groups

Using your Bibles or concordances, work together to find Scriptures that refer to trust. List them in the space below, and then write them on the newsprint sheet to act as bridges between ideas.

Your Trust Web may look something like this:

keeps his word
promises answer to prayer
sent Jesus for salvation

pray
read Bible
follow God's will

1 Corinthians 10:12-13

Trust in God

death
illness
temptation

Genesis 22:15-18

Genesis 6:18

Noah
Abraham
Ruth

On your own, look at the Trust Web and write a response to the following question:

• Do you see any ideas that you believe can help strengthen your trust in God?

Share your thoughts with your group.

To trust in God and follow his will, you have to take time to listen to him. There is great power in prayer. With your group, read the following Scriptures about trust and prayer. Decide on the main idea of each Scripture, and write it on the line next to that Scripture.

• Psalm 52:7-8 _____

• Matthew 21:22 _____

• John 14:1-4 _____

• Philippians 4:6-7 _____

• Philippians 4:13 _____

In the space below, write any of the Scriptures that you really like or that really touch you emotionally or spiritually.

With a partner, read Psalm 46:10a. Take a few minutes for quiet meditation with your partner, thinking about the Scriptures you've read and meditating on God's greatness. Pray that you will know his will for your life and that you may always trust in him

Leader Instructions

After groups have created the four lists, have one volunteer stand at the Trust Web and draw connecting lines between ideas (make each connecting line a different color). As the groups direct him or her, have the volunteer connect items at the top of the sheet to items at the bottom of the sheet. For example, if the group wrote "Noah" as a person who trusted in God, have the volunteer draw a connecting line from Noah to "keeps his word" to show that God showed Noah he was trustworthy. Do the same to connect items on the left and right sides of the sheet.

After groups have finished the Trust Web, process the experience using questions such as these:

- How can you put the Lord first in your life?
- How can you tell that you are following God's will?

Extension Idea

After completing the Trust Web, if you have time and feel creative, write (or have students write) a leader-guided meditation to close your class time. Base the meditation on the Scriptures listed at the bottom of the Trust Web page (p. 39). Use the leader-guided meditation instead of the individual meditation time.

Apply It

Trusting in the Lord means following his will. But we often don't know what God's will for us might be, since he usually doesn't speak to us in an audible voice. Wouldn't it be nice if he whispered clearly in your ear, "Mary, get off your duff and go enroll in seminary!"

Read these five steps for discerning the will of God from *Life on the Edge* by Dr. James Dobson:

1. Pray for spiritual wisdom and insight. Read Ephesians 1:17-18.
2. Examine the Scriptures for principles that relate to your issue.
3. Seek advice from a counselor or a pastor who is spiritually mature and solid in his or her faith.
4. Pay close attention to what is known as "providential circumstances." The Lord often speaks through doors that open or close.
5. Do nothing impulsively. Give God an opportunity to speak.

And finally, follow the words of Mark 16:15b—God's general will for all believers—"Go into all the world and preach the good news to all creation."

With a partner, discuss these statements or questions:

- Share a time you've felt God was speaking to you or telling you to do something.
- Did you trust in God enough to follow him? Explain.

- Can you think of a time God shut one door and opened another for you or a family member?

With your partner, share an area of your life in which you'd like to know God's will for you, or an area in which you're looking for some guidance. In the space below, write specifically how Dr. Dobson's steps may help you discover God's will. With your partner, commit to following these steps to find direction. Then commit to remind each other to look back at this book in a few months to see what happened in the area in which you were seeking to know God's will.

_____

_____

_____

Live It

Read Psalm 62.

- What's your favorite verse in this psalm? Why? Copy your favorite verse onto a sheet of paper, and hang it in your room where you can see it often.

_____

_____

- In this psalm, God is compared to a rock, a refuge, and a fortress. How might this be a comfort? How has God been a refuge for you during bad times in your life?

_____

_____

- In order to give God your total trust and faithfulness, you have to be more "God-focused" than self-focused. How can you move in this direction?

_____

_____

_____

Tell Me More...

Sometimes when bad things happen in our lives, our trust in God wavers. When people lose a loved one, suffer one hardship after another, or nothing seems to go right in their lives, they might think God has abandoned them or they may blame him for their troubles.

But Scripture tells us to trust in God even when we don't understand—when there is no answer or logical explanation for why people suffer from war, disasters, or disease.

Dr. James Dobson writes in *Life on the Edge* about the sovereignty of God: "If you believe God is obligated to explain himself to us, you ought to examine the Scripture."

He cites 1 Corinthians 2:11b, which says, "No one knows the thoughts of God except the Spirit of God," and Isaiah 55:8-9: " 'For my thoughts are not your thoughts, neither are your ways my ways,' declares the Lord. 'As the heavens are higher than the earth, so are my ways higher than your ways and my thoughts than your thoughts.'"

"Clearly Scripture tells us we lack the capacity to grasp God's infinite mind or the way he intervenes in our lives," Dobson says. "What this means in practical terms is that many of our questions—especially those that begin with the word 'why'—will have to remain unanswered for the time being."

In 1 Corinthians 13:12, Paul writes that we will understand fully when we see God face to face.

Our God is a loving and kind God. And when bad things happen or your burdens become too great—trust in him and pray. Pray for strength to carry on, for wisdom to understand, for friends to help you, and for peaceful thoughts.

"Ask and it will be given to you; seek and you will find; knock and the door will be opened to you. For everyone who asks receives; he who seeks finds; and to him who knocks, the door will be opened" (Matthew 7:7-8).

A Generous Spirit

 God shows us the way to be generous.

Supplies: You'll need Bibles, pens or pencils, newsprint, and markers.

Preparation: On a table, set out the supplies to use during the study.

Leader Instructions

Begin by having students each read the "Read About It" section and respond in the "Write About It" section.

Read About It

Commenting on the idea of generosity in the Sermon on the Mount, John Stott notes:

> Generosity is not enough, however. Our Lord is concerned throughout this Sermon with motivation, with the hidden thoughts of the heart...
>
> The question is not so much what the hand is doing (passing over some cash or a check) but what the heart is thinking while the hand is doing it. There are three possibilities. Either we are seeking the praise of men, or we preserve our anonymity but are quietly congratulating ourselves, or we are desirous of the approval of our divine father alone.
>
> (John R.W. Stott, *The Message of the Sermon on the Mount,*
> as quoted in *Disciplines for the Inner Life*)

Praise seeking. Hypocritical giving. Divine approval. Generosity flows *from* somewhere, and it flows to somewhere. It's essential to remember that no matter what you give or how you give it, it affects someone. If you give a candy bar to a starving child, that child will have something to fill his or her stomach while being affected by your action and obedience. Thus, the challenge to be generous has two distinct parts: First, we must give with the right motives, and second, we must respond to God's call to give what we can whenever he asks.

Write About It

- We can define "generosity" in many ways. Below, write your definition:

_____

_____

_____

- The reading gives three reasons to be generous. Read them again, and circle the one that best describes what fuels your generosity. Why did you choose that reason?

_____

_____

_____

- How might your generosity change other people's lives? How might it change your own life?

_____

_____

_____

- Read Psalm 139:23-24. Before you continue this study, write a prayer to God asking him to search you and reveal to you the type of generosity he wants from you.

_____

_____

_____

Experience It

Leader Instructions

Have students form four groups, and point out the supply table you've prepared before the study.

In your group, follow the instructions on the "Understanding Generosity" page (pp. 45-47). Use the supplies on the supply table as needed.

Understanding Generosity
Section 1

Read Mark 12:41-44. As a group, discuss the following questions and write the answers in the spaces provided:

• Why is it significant that this woman gave out of her poverty? Was she being generous? Explain.

_____

_____

• What did Jesus' response to this situation say about the importance of generosity?

_____

_____

• Is it possible to give a lot of money and still not be generous? Explain.

_____

_____

• How much should people be willing to give in order to be considered "generous"?

_____

_____

Using the space provided, work together to write a monologue from the widow's perspective. Include her thoughts on her poverty, her perspective on God's provision, and reasons she might have given what she did.

_____

_____

_____

When you've finished, get together with the members of another group and read your monologue to them. Then discuss this question in your group, and write the answer in the space provided:

• What did you learn about the woman from writing your monologue?

_____

_____

Section 2

Read Luke 9:10-17. As a group, discuss the following questions and write the answers in the spaces provided:

• What did Jesus demonstrate about God's generosity in this passage?

_____

_____

• What is significant about the fact that there was food left over?

_____

_____

• When have you experienced God's generosity in your own life? Explain.

_____

_____

As a group, create a short skit about a fictional character who was in the crowd that Jesus fed. Include how the person might have felt about having his or her lunch provided by God and how others in the crowd might have reacted to what was happening. Be sure to include everyone from your group in the skit. When you've finished, perform your skit for the rest of the class. Then discuss these questions in your group, and write the answers in the spaces provided:
• What did you discover about people's reactions to being the recipients of generosity?

_____

_____

• What is so important about what Jesus did?

_____

_____

• How can we model Jesus' behavior?

_____

_____

Section 3

Read Matthew 6:1-4. As a group, discuss the following questions and write the answers in the spaces provided:
• What does this passage say about our attitude when we give?

_____

_____

about God's reaction when we give?

_____

_____

• Why does God want us to keep our giving quiet?

_____

_____

As a group, make a list of people who might need you to give to them. Be sure to include people who need more than just money.

_____

_____

When you've finished, discuss this question and write the answer in the space provided:
• How would Jesus give to these people?

_____

_____

Section 4

Read 2 Corinthians 9:6-15. As a group, discuss the following questions and write the answers in the spaces provided:
• What does this passage tell us about God's generosity?

_____

about our responsibility in giving?

_____

_____

about the results of our giving?

_____

_____

about God's response when we give?

_____

_____

As a group, use the newsprint and markers to create an illustration of this passage. Consider including the following: a person giving and his or her reaction, a person receiving and his or her reaction, and God's perspective on the process of giving and receiving. When you've finished, discuss these questions in your group and write the answers in the spaces provided.
• When we give, should we consider the results of our giving?

_____

_____

• Is it OK to give to others because we think God will bless us with more things to give? Explain.

_____

_____

• If you had very little to give, what would you think if God asked you to give generously? How should you deal with those emotions?

_____

_____

After groups have finished the "Understanding Generosity" page, process the experience using questions such as these:

- What are the most challenging things about being generous?
- After completing this experience, do you think you need to change your attitude or actions about being generous?

Tell Me More...

"You must give what will cost you something. This, then, is giving not just what you can live without but what you can't live without or don't want to live without, something you really like. Then your gift becomes a sacrifice, which will have value before God."

(Mother Teresa, *A Simple Path*)

Apply It

Find a partner, and read to him or her the prayer you wrote at the beginning of this study. Then discuss some of the things that you've learned about generosity through this study.

Clockwise, from upper left to lower left, label the four sections of the "Squaring Off With Generosity" page (p. 50) in the following order: "The best thing about generosity," "The hardest thing about generosity," "What I need to give," and "When I'm going to apply these principles." Work silently on your own to complete the page.

When you've finished, share what you've written with your partner. Then spend time praying about the things you've committed to on your handouts. When you've finished praying, exchange phone numbers with your partner and commit to following up twice during the next week to see how your partner is doing with the commitments he or she has made.

Live It

- Make a list of every possession that is important to you.

_____

_____

_____

- Spend time praying about which of these things God might want you to give away.
- Think about the following statement, and write your response in the space provided: "God wants me to live a life of generosity."

_____

_____

_____

• Think of two people who have succeeded at generosity. Find those people, and spend time learning the difficulties they've faced trying to be generous. Hearing their struggles and seeing how they live will give you insight into ways you can apply this principle to your own life.

Tell Me More...

Here's a common dialogue that often happens between us and God:

Us: I've got all these wonderful things. I'm so blessed. I think I'll let these things provide security for me and boost my self-esteem.

God: I gave you those things. You need to give some of them away.

Us: But God, these things are important to me. And besides, I *need* these things. I might not make it without them.

God: Who created you? Who created the things that sustain you? Give me a break! Give 'em away.

Us: But God! How will I survive?!

It's so easy to hold onto the things that God has provided. And it's just as easy to rely on the things God provides rather than to rely on God.

So what's important to remember? We've got to always listen to what God wants us to do with what he's provided. If he says, "Give it away," then we've got to do it. What other response could we have to the request of the One who gave us everything we have?

Squaring Off With Generosity

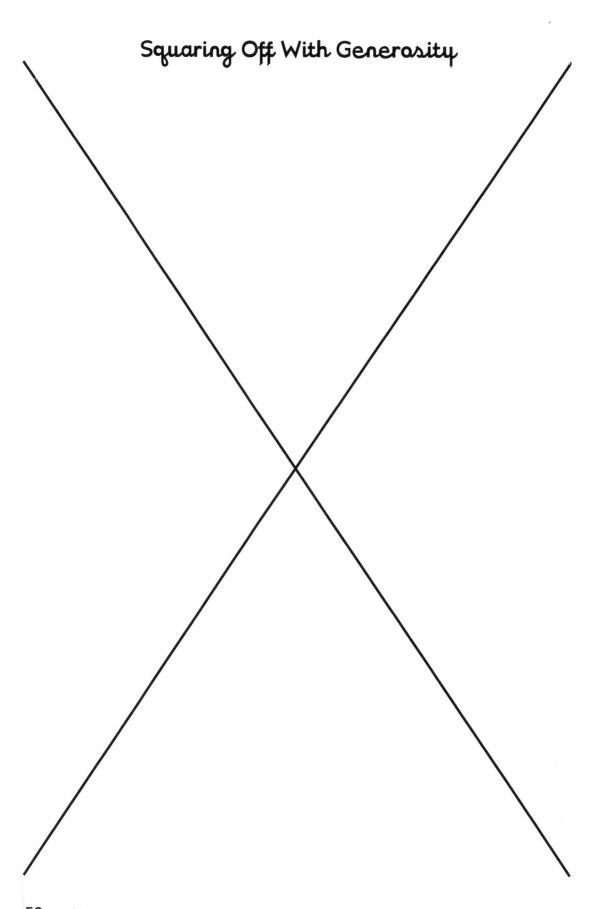

The Heart of Compassion

The Bible shows us how to live compassionate lives.

Supplies: You'll need Bibles, pens or pencils, newsprint, and markers.

Preparation: On a table, set out the supplies to use during the study.

Leader Instructions

Begin by having students read the "Read About It" section and respond in the "Write About It" section.

Read About It

The Samaritan listened carefully as, with silent nudges, he guided his donkey along the dusty road. This was the part of the journey he dreaded most. Here the highway narrowed to little more than a path, curving around boulders and disappearing into thick brush. If there were robbers, this is where they would be waiting, hoping for the chance to pick off a lone traveler.

"Well," thought the Samaritan, touching the hilt of his knife, "I might be alone, but I'm no easy target."

And that's when he saw the man—bloodied, beaten, all but stripped naked, and lying face down in the ditch.

The man was a Jew. Maybe he was one of the merchants the Samaritan had met in Jerusalem—men who thought nothing of cheating Samaritans. Or maybe he was one of the priests who'd brushed past the Samaritan without so much as a sideways glance.

The Samaritan paused, looking down into the battered face. The robbers might still be near. They might at that moment be watching him, hoping he'd dismount and step off the road into the shadows.

The dying man was a *Jew,* no friend of Samaritans. If the situation were reversed, the Samaritan knew the man probably would not stop to help—not now, not ever.

What to do?

Write About It

• If you'd been the Samaritan facing this decision, what would you have decided? Why?

_____

_____

_____

• The Samaritan had the opportunity to express compassion to the robbery victim. How would you define compassion?

_____

_____

_____

• Describe a time you've experienced compassion—either giving it or receiving it.

_____

_____

_____

Experience It

Read Luke 10:30-35. Notice that the Samaritan did more than simply administer first aid (oil, wine, and bandages were medicine at the time). The Samaritan also paid for the wounded man's lodging.

All this for an unknown Jewish man whose people systematically discriminated against Samaritans.

Assume you're the man who was beaten. You've come to in the inn, and the innkeeper has explained what happened to you. The innkeeper has also explained that an unknown Samaritan is footing the bill for your recovery.

You decide to write a letter to your family to explain what's happened and where you are.

In your letter, you decide to explain why this Samaritan did what he did.

Take a few minutes to write that letter now.

_____

_____

_____

Now join with two others, and share what you've written. See where you agree and where your letters differ. Discuss these questions in your trio:

• How did you explain your good fortune?
• How did you describe the Samaritan?
• How did you explain the Samaritan's kindness toward you?

It's been said that opportunities to be compassionate are endless, but we don't see them because we've trained ourselves not to see them and not to get involved.

It's time to identify a few opportunities.

Find a new partner, and take a few minutes to do the following:

• Compare your definitions of compassion. Come to an agreement regarding what it means to be compassionate. Write what you've agreed on here:

Now for your challenge: With your partner, take ten minutes to find at least one specific opportunity to be compassionate. You don't have to actually do a compassionate act, but do identify at least one. Try to identify three or more. Rejoin the group in ten minutes or less.

Leader Instructions

Help students catch the vision by pointing out that opportunities for compassion might be right in the room. Someone might have a car that needs repair—but the driver can't afford it. If you meet in a church building, you might identify people in the congregation who could use compassion in their lives.

If all else fails, ask pairs to stand on a corner watching traffic pass and discussing what they see. Is there someone who could benefit from a specific compassionate act, such as the driver of a van with handicapped license plates, a young mother attempting to drive as three children squabble, or the driver of a moving van coming into the neighborhood?

Leader Instructions

Keep a running list of compassionate acts on a piece of newsprint. The list will be helpful later.

When everyone has reassembled, have everyone share ideas for compassionate acts with the larger group. Discuss these questions as a group:

• Many needs are obvious—why doesn't someone do something to help?

• What would it cost to be compassionate in the ways you've identified?

• If the Samaritan described in Jesus' parable witnessed the needs you just saw, what do you think the Samaritan would do? Why?

• What has it cost for God to be compassionate to you?

Read Romans 5:6-8, and discuss this question:

• Given this cost of God's compassion for us, what acts of compassion that you've identified are too demanding or expensive for you?

Tell Me More...

Samaria was the land between Judea and Galilee. Jews regarded Samaritans as outsiders who compromised their race and culture through mixed marriages and temple worship away from Jerusalem. (See 2 Kings 17:24-34.)

Apply It

Here's the thing about compassion: you're already involved. If you've accepted Jesus as Lord, you've *received* compassion.

The question is—are you *giving* compassion?

Compassion isn't about being fair or giving people what they deserve. It's about empathizing and sympathizing with others—and jumping in to help even when no one has a claim on your efforts. It's a gift.

Compassion sometimes appears to be a dying art, but in the kingdom of God, compassion is essential—both feeling it and acting on it.

Read the following passages. Answer these questions for each one:

• How does compassion fit into the kingdom of God?

• What does God expect of you?

• What has God shown you about compassion?

Psalm 145:9

Mark 1:40-42

_____

_____

_____

2 Corinthians 1:3-4

_____

_____

_____

Colossians 3:12-14

_____

_____

 ## Extension Idea

Draft two "instant actors" to act out the following story as you read it.

The Pretty Nice, but Totally Ineffective, Samaritan

A young man walked quickly along a busy Manhattan sidewalk. Late for a job interview, he checked his watch as he darted in and out of the thick pedestrian traffic.

Then he saw her.

Up ahead, an elderly woman stood near the curb, leaning on a wooden cane. She peered uncertainly through thick glasses, staring at the honking traffic as if waiting for cars to stop and let her cross. She raised the cane and waved it, as if scolding the drivers would prompt them to let an ancient woman slowly shuffle across the boulevard.

The young man sighed, glanced at his watch, and stopped next to the woman. He took her gently by the elbow and, without a word, expertly guided her safely across the noisy street.

When they were safe on the far curb, the woman asked the man for his name as she pulled out her wallet. "Bob Thompson," he said, "but put your wallet away. I don't want a reward."

The woman slipped a piece of paper and the stub of a pencil out of her wallet. She wrote the man's name in a thin, shaking hand. "Reward?" she warbled angrily, "I'm going to report you. You kidnapped me just when my taxi was pulling up. Now I've got to walk the twenty blocks uptown!"

Discuss these questions as a group:

- *What's the moral of this story?*
- *Why did Bob's compassion create a problem rather than a solution?*

One moral of this story might be this: When we fail to listen, our involvement sometimes makes situations worse rather than better.

- *Do you know someone who is an excellent listener? What things make him or her an excellent listener?*
- *How is listening well an act of compassion?*

Pair up with a new partner, and review what you've written. Discuss these questions:

- How are your answers alike? How are they different?
- What conclusions can you draw about compassion from what you've read in Scripture?
- How have you shown compassion to another person?
- In what ways have you received compassion?

In your pair, select the compassionate act from the newsprint that is most intriguing to you. Discuss these questions:

- How could you respond to the identified need?
- What resources would you need?
- What are the barriers to being actively compassionate in this way?
- What are the opportunities for being actively compassionate in this way?
- Will you do something to address this need? If so, describe what you'll do below:

- When will you do this?

- What's the first step? the next step? Sketch out your plan:

Plans are only worthwhile if they're consistent with God's will. You've seen how God encourages compassion—so your compassionate act is clearly within God's will.

But it's easy to get focused on the *task* and forget the *reason* behind it.

With your partner, prayerfully dedicate your compassionate act to God. Ask for God's guidance as you work through your plan. Ask for God's eyes as you see needs and respond to them. Ask for flexibility.

Then praise God for demonstrating compassion to you.

Live It

In the next few days, look for compassion in action. Skim newspapers. Watch the news.

Where do you see "compassion with skin on it"? Who's serving, caring, and active? How well-represented is the church in compassionate service?

- If Christians seem to be underrepresented, what do you intend to do about it?

_____

_____

_____

- If Christians are among those serving, how can you support them?

_____

_____

_____

Tell Me More...

Why didn't the priest or the Levite stop to help the wounded man?

In Jesus' parable, the priest and the Levite represent Jewish religious leadership. Priests helped in temple worship, and Levites were lay associates of priests and often served in the temple. Both men were obviously concerned about ritual purity, and touching a dead or dying man would have made them unclean. By avoiding the wounded man, they insulated themselves from being tainted—but they also kept themselves from showing compassion.

It was not lost on Jesus' audience that he valued compassion and involvement more than he valued ritualistic purity.

Semper Fidelis
(Always Faithful)

 God shows us how to live faithful lives.

Supplies: You'll need Bibles, pens or pencils, pipe cleaners, and envelopes.

Preparation: Prepare envelopes with pipe cleaners in them as described in the "Experience It" section. On a table, set out the supplies to use during the study.

Leader Instructions

Begin by having students each read the "Read About It" section and respond in the "Write About It" section.

Read About It

Outside the gate of Rome on the Appian Way, which leads southward to the seaports, stands a building known as the Chapel of the Quo Vadis. It commemorates a legend about the Apostle Peter. When the persecution by Nero was at its height, Simon Peter was urged by the Christians to escape from the city. He complied with their insistence and was fleeing toward safety, when he saw a mysterious figure approaching him. As the person drew nearer, he recognized Jesus, and said to him in Latin, "Quo vadis, Domine? [Where are you going, Lord?]"

Back came the answer: "I am going to Rome to be crucified again, because my servant Peter is leaving the church."

With tears of repentance and shame, Peter turned back to Rome, and went to his death. The chapel marks the place where the interview supposedly occurred.

It is always too early to turn away from Jesus. His message to the world is transmitted not by those who know about him and leave him, but by those who know him and stay with him.

(Merrill C. Tenney, *Who's Boss?*)

Write About It

• What does this story tell you about Peter?

_____

_____

_____

- Read Luke 22:31-34, 54-62. How does the Bible's portrayal of Peter fit with the story you read about him?

_____

_____

_____

- Are you sometimes like Peter? If so, how?

_____

_____

_____

- Read 1 John 5:3-5. According to this Scripture, how can we "win" in life?

_____

_____

_____

Experience It

Leader Instructions

Prepare an envelope for each person. In one-third of the envelopes, place one pipe cleaner; in one-third place two pipe cleaners; and in one-third place five pipe cleaners. Distribute the envelopes, and tell students to follow the instructions below. Don't try to define the task any more than what's written. After students have finished, have each show what he or she has made. Then have them journal their thoughts in answer to the questions that follow.

Using what's in your envelope, make something of significance. You have five minutes.

After showing what you've made, answer the following questions:

- How faithful were you to the instructions you were given? Explain.

_____

_____

_____

Extension Idea

Instead of using pipe cleaners, make this activity more interesting by giving students varying amounts of art or craft supplies.

• Was it easy or difficult to be faithful to the instructions? Explain.

_____

_____

_____

• What was it like to receive more or less than others received?

_____

_____

_____

• Did the people with more or with less have a greater challenge? a greater responsibility? Explain.

_____

_____

_____

• Did having little totally prohibit people from making something significant? Why or why not?

_____

_____

_____

Form groups of about four, and read aloud Matthew 25:14-30. Then discuss the following questions in your group. Jot your group's conclusions under each question.

• How was your activity with the pipe cleaners similar to what happened in this passage?

_____

_____

_____

• Why do you think the first two servants were given more than they'd originally been given? How is that like our relationship with God?

_____

_____

_____

Tell Me More...

"Success is to be measured not by wealth, power, or fame, but by the ratio between what a man is and what he might be."

—H.G. Wells

- The third servant did nothing illegal or "wrong." What was it about his actions that resulted in punishment?

_____

_____

_____

- What did the master expect of the servants? What does God expect of us?

_____

_____

_____

- If you feel you've been given less ability, intelligence, or opportunity than others, does that mean God won't expect as much from you? Explain.

_____

_____

_____

- In this parable, what is Jesus teaching about how to live a faithful life?

_____

_____

After your group discussion, report your most interesting insights to the rest of the class.

Tell Me More...

"Consider it pure joy, my brothers, whenever you face trials of many kinds, because you know that the testing of your faith develops perseverance. Perseverance must finish its work so that you may be mature and complete, not lacking anything" (James 1:2-4).

Apply It

Think about what it means to live a faithful life. Be sure to think about the message of today's Bible passage.

- Who or what should you be faithful to? Without consulting others, list as many as you can think of.

_____

_____

When you've completed your list, form a group with two or three other people. In your group, compare your lists of who or what you should be faithful to and choose the top four or five people or things you can agree on. List them below:

_____

_____

_____

Leader Instructions

With your partner, determine ways you can practically live out your faithfulness to the object of faithfulness you've been assigned. For example, if you want to live out faithfulness to God, you might suggest developing a regular quiet time in which you seek to know God better. Write your suggestions below:

_____

_____

_____

When you've come up with all the ideas you can, share them with the rest of the class. Listen as other groups share, and think about ways we can see that God wants us to live faithful lives. Choose three ways you want to work on becoming more faithful in your life, and in the space below, list those three in order of their priority:

1. _____

2. _____

3. _____

Extension Idea

Make a list of the ideas for becoming more faithful as pairs share them with the class. The next time you meet, pull out the list and ask how students are doing with living faithful lives.

Now think about what it would look like, sound like, and feel like if you really followed through on the first priority you've listed. Draw or describe that in the space below:

Tell Me More...

"Our relationship to our heavenly Father, though secure, is not static. He wants his children to grow up to know him more and more intimately. Generations of Christians have discovered that the principal way to do so is to wait upon him every day in a time of Bible reading and prayer. This is an indispensable necessity for the Christian who wants to make progress. We are all busy nowadays, but we must somehow rearrange our priorities in order to make time for it. It will mean rigorous self-discipline, but granted this, together with a legible Bible and an alarm clock that works, we are well on the road to victory."

(John R.W. Stott, *Basic Christianity*)

Now trade books with your partner, and pray for your partner in the three areas he or she listed. Alternate praying with your partner, beginning with the third priority and working up to the first for both of you. Ask God to help both of you follow through on your commitments.

Live It

• Read Hebrews 12:1-2. Why is it important that we remain faithful to God?

_____

_____

_____

• What does it mean to remain faithful to God?

_____

_____

_____

• Read 1 Corinthians 12:14-27. Why is it important that we remain faithful to the church?

_____

_____

_____

• What does it mean to remain faithful to the church?

_____

_____

_____

• Read Matthew 5:33-37. Why is it important that we remain faithful to our word?

_____

_____

_____

• What does it mean to remain faithful to our word?

_____

_____

_____

Tell Me More...

"Isabella Baumfree was an African-American slave born to a Dutch owner in Ulster County, New York, about 1797. She was separated from her family and sold twice before she was twelve. Slave life was never easy. Even after she was set free in 1827, she barely survived as a domestic helper in New York City.

"After the Civil War began, Isabella left New York to 'travel up an' down the land showin' the people their sins an' bein' a sign unto them.' She even changed her name to Sojourner Truth.

"Sojourner Truth became famous for her unique style of preaching. Although she couldn't read or write, she preached a message of freedom for slaves, women, and the poor. She spoke in a heavy Dutch accent, knew the Bible well, and drew stares by wrapping a turban around her head.

"Because blacks—especially black women—were routinely oppressed, Sojourner Truth found the going difficult. But she kept at it, hardened by her life of slavery and struggle. Her fame spread; she even met with President Lincoln in 1864.

"Fame doesn't always equal popularity, as Sojourner Truth found out. She often preached and lectured before hostile audiences. Many times she was told her mission was hopeless.'"I don't care any more for your talk than I do for the bite of a flea,' someone told her.

" 'Perhaps not,' she replied, 'but the Lord willing, I'll keep you scratchin'.' "

(The Youth Bible)

Sojourner Truth remained faithful by taking what little she'd been given and using it to tell people about Jesus, no matter how difficult the circumstances.